Ian Beck's

HOME
Before
DARK

For Lily, Edmund and Laurence.

Teddy Bears have such a quiet life,
don't they?

Scholastic Children's Books,
Commonwealth House, 1-19 New Oxford Street,
London WC1A 1NU, UK
a division of Scholastic Ltd

London ~ New York ~ Toronto ~ Sydney ~ Auckland
Mexico City ~ New Delhi ~ Hong Kong

Published by Scholastic Ltd, 1997

Text and illustrations copyright © Ian Beck, 1997

ISBN 0 590 54227 X (Hardback)
ISBN 0 590 19918 8 (Paperback)

Printed and bound in China

Teddy was sitting alone on the stairs. Lily and her Mum were getting ready to go out.

"Wait," said Lily. "We can't go yet, we nearly forgot Teddy. Poor old thing, he thought he was left behind."

"Oooh, it's windy," said Mum. "I'm glad we're wrapped up warm."
"Teddy likes going to the park," said Lily.

They stayed a long time in the park. They played on the swings, and they fed the ducks.

"It's getting late," said Mum, "and I think
it might rain. Come on, we must get home
before dark."

Lily was so tired she fell asleep. She cuddled
Teddy but . . . Oh no, poor Teddy, Lily
dropped him!

And so Mum and Lily set off home
without Teddy.

Teddy was left all alone.

He walked up to the dark iron railings.

And he pushed, and squeezed, and squashed up his tummy until . . .

. . . he was through. But out on the
pavement he felt VERY small.

He was very careful. He crossed at the
crossing and remembered to look both ways.

Oh dear! A big car splashed him all over.

On the pavement he was kicked and jostled
and bashed and bumped, by all the boots and
shoes and bags and shopping.

Then it began to rain. And the rain came down harder and harder.

Teddy had to shelter by a dustbin. A great, big, hairy dog came and sniffed at him.

Teddy thought that he would never
see Lily again.

"I MUST get home before dark. That's when Lily needs me the most." So bravely he set off up the hill against the wind and the rain.

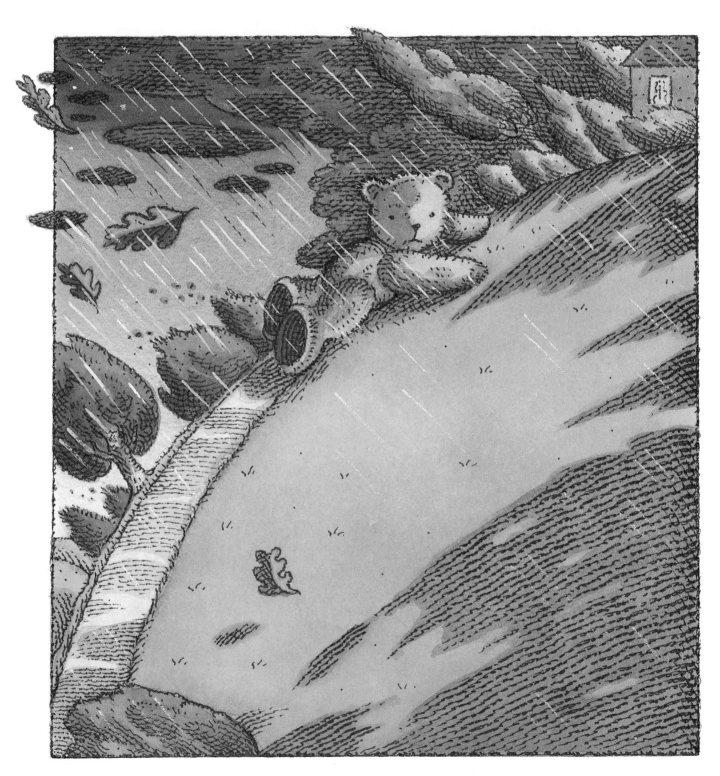

It was a very, very, VERY steep hill. By the time he reached the top, it was nearly dark.

And it was a very, very, VERY strong wind.

"WHOOSH!" went the wind. Head over heels he tumbled, down and over, over and down, all the way to his house.

He tried to tap at the door with his cold, wet paws, but no one could hear him.

And so out in the dark, he waited, and waited,
and waited . . .

Until a friendly voice said, "You poor old bear, have they forgotten you? Never mind, I know what to do."

And so the paperboy delivered Teddy through the letter box, into the warmth and safety of the buggy seat.

At bedtime, Lily said, "Where's Teddy? I can't go to bed without him. Ah, here he is. You have an easy life, don't you Teddy?"

Good Night Lily. Kiss, kiss.
And Good Night, Teddy. Sleep tight.
But *we* know what really happened, don't we?